For my little flower.

BIG GIRL

GIRL

potty

By Mary Lee

Pee

Poop

When I need to go, I use the potty.

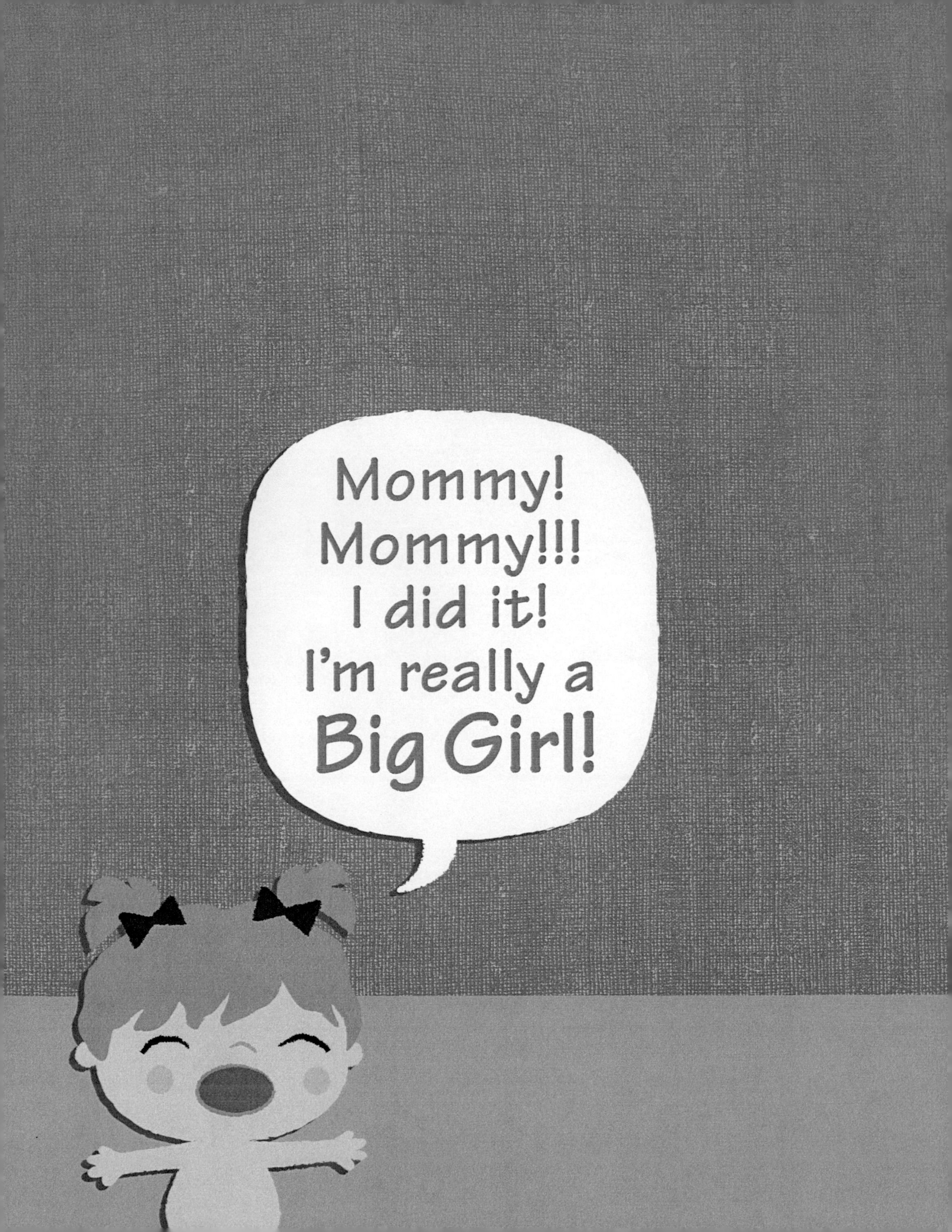
Mommy!
Mommy!!!
I did it!
I'm really a
Big Girl!

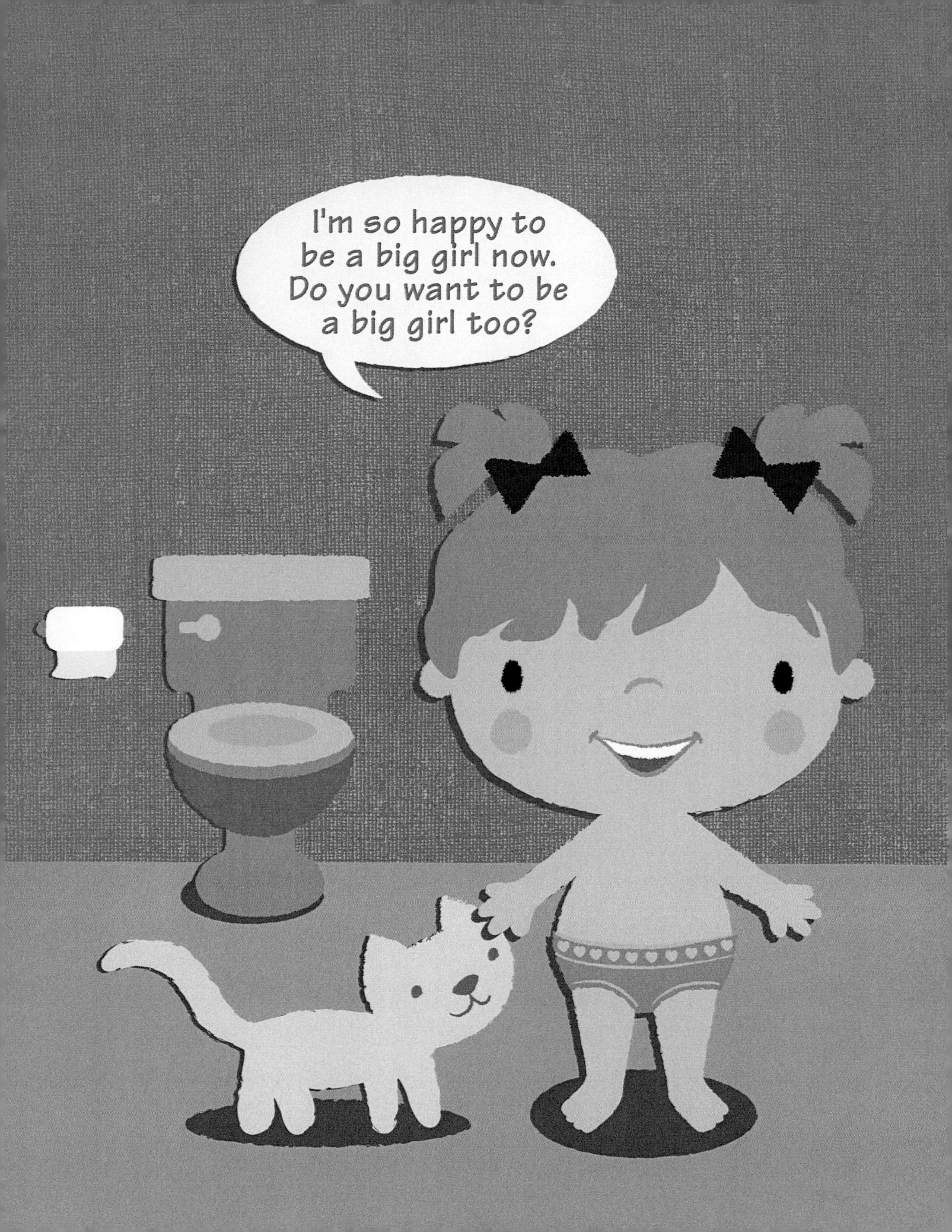
I'm so happy to be a big girl now. Do you want to be a big girl too?

3 Little Potty Training Tips:

1. **Don't stress.** They're not likely to go to college in diapers. Nothing lasts forever.

2. **Don't worry.** Just because you read about someone who potty-trained their baby at four months old doesn't mean that can work for everyone. The pace is different for every child.

3. **Do give yourself a break.** You have one of the hardest jobs in the world. You deserve a pat on the back and maybe a spa day once in a while.

Find more books by Mary Lee at
www.maryleekids.blogspot.com